GALAXY WARS

by
Tracey West

CHOLASTIC INC.

K TORONTO LONDON AUCKLAND
EXICO CITY NEW DELHI HONG KONG

No part of this work may be reproduced in whole or in part, or stored in a retrieval system, or transmitted in any form or by any means, electronic, mechanical, photocopying, recording, or otherwise, without written permission of the publisher. For information regarding permission, write to Scholastic Inc., Attention: Permissions Department, 557 Broadway, New York, NY 10012.

ISBN 978-0-545-22252-5

CARTOON NETWORK, the logo, Ben 10 Ultra Alien, and all related characters and elements are trademarks of and © 2010 Cartoon Network. Published by Scholastic Inc.
SCHOLASTIC and associated logos are trademarks and/or registered trademarks of Scholastic Inc.

12 11 10 9 8 7 6 5 4 3 2 1   10 11 12 13 14 15/0

Designed by Rick DeMonico
Printed in the U.S.A.   40
First printing, August 2010

No fair! You moved your Pupa an extra space!"

Cumo frowned across the table at his game partner, Cirro. The two tech specialists were on duty at the Intergalactic Communications Center in the orbit of Ventulus, a planet on the outer rim of the Morpho galaxy. Although they were members of the Hedillan species, they were very much like other workers all over the universe. Things were slow, and they were goofing off.

Nothing much ever happened at the comm station anyway. Although Ventulus was a technologically advanced planet, the Hedillans who populated it were happy with the way things were, and didn't do much space traveling. They had a no-trade policy with other planets as well, so when alien ships came into Ventulus space, they were told very politely to turn around and go home. If that didn't work, the Hedillans used their arsenal of laser cannons to get the point across.

Word got around the galaxy that the Hedillans didn't want any visitors, so the comm station was almost always quiet. Cumo and Cirro were there to fix things that malfunctioned and field any messages that came in.

Most of the time, they played their favorite board game, Existence. The object of the game was to get to the end with the most money and awards for good citizenship. Cirro always won, and Cumo was getting pretty tired of it. He was sure Cirro must be cheating.

"You're seeing things," Cirro told him.

"My eyes are fine," Cumo snapped. Like all Hedillans, his large, black eyes were the largest features on his face. His antennae twitched in annoyance. "You're cheating! I know it!"

Cirro flapped his pale white wings, a sign he was getting angry. "I am not! Now take your turn!"

Beep! Beep! Beep! Beep!

"Did you say something?" Cirro asked.

"That wasn't me," Cumo replied. His eyes rotated so he could see behind him. "Well, look at that! It's the radar! We've got company."

Both workers wheeled their metal chairs over to their station. The radar screen showed a large blip moving toward Ventulus. Cirro pressed a button on the control panel in front of him.

"You are entering Ventulus space," he announced. "Please turn around immediately. There are no visitors allowed here."

There was no reply. Cumo went to another screen and started twisting dials.

"I've got a visual," he said. "It's a Pratarian ship!"

"Those ground dwellers?" Cirro asked. "I wonder what brought them out of their holes?"

"They must not have heard you," Cumo said. "Try again."

"Repeat, you are about to enter Ventulus space," Cirro said. "Do not proceed."

But the ship kept coming.

"What do we do now?" Cumo asked.

Cirro flipped through the comm station manual. "It says here to activate the laser cannons."

"Laser cannons?" Cumo asked. "That seems a bit

harsh, doesn't it? I mean, maybe they just can't hear us, or—"

BOOM! An explosion rocked the comm station, throwing Cumo and Cirro off of their chairs. They groaned and looked at each other, stunned.

"We're under attack!" Cirro yelled. "Raise the shields!"

Cumo jumped up and frantically pressed buttons on his station. "The shields are down," he reported, his voice rising in panic. "They've been disabled!"

BOOM! Another explosion hit the station. Cumo went flying back against the wall. Cirro ran to him and grabbed his arm.

"We've got to get out of here," he said.

"Right!" Cumo agreed. "The escape pods."

They raced through the comm station, through smoke and sparks, to get to the transport bay. Luckily, the escape pods were easy to get to. They each jumped in one as another blast of fire assaulted the station.

Within seconds they were whipping away from the comm station and racing toward the planet's surface. Cirro made contact with the Hedillan command center.

"General, we are under attack!" he cried. "It's a Pratarian ship."

Cumo's eyes rotated just in time to see the comm station blow up in a spectacle of fire and light.

"The comm station has been destroyed," Cumo reported.

On the planet's surface, the Hedillan general began activating the laser cannons. Behind him, Monarch, the Hedillan ruler, seethed with fury.

"The Pratarians will rue the day they attacked Ventulus," he said. "This is war!"

CHAPTER ONE

Woo hoo! It's party time!" Ben Tennyson said, climbing out of his car. His sometimes-girlfriend, Julie Yamamoto, got out of the passenger seat next to him.

A tall boy with shaggy brown hair emerged from the backseat. "Can somebody remind me again what we're doing here?" Kevin Levin asked.

Gwen Tennyson got out of the car last. "Come on, Kevin, it won't be so bad," said the red-haired teen. She had the same green eyes as her cousin, Ben. "Cooper did help us save Earth once. The least we can do is go to his sixteenth birthday party."

"I didn't know nerds knew how to party," Kevin mumbled.

Ben shrugged. "Hey, I'm not thrilled about this either, but how bad can it be?"

"I spent two days in jail on Athos chained to a methane monster," Kevin replied. "I'm guessing that was more fun than this is going to be."

Julie patted the head of the small creature in her arms. Ship was a Galvanic Mechomorph that could transform into any technological device. His normal form was that of a vaguely dog-shaped creature without any face, ears, or fur. His shiny black body was marked with neon-green stripes.

"I hope Cooper's mom doesn't mind pets," Julie said.

"She raised Cooper, didn't she?" Kevin joked.

Gwen punched him lightly in the arm. "Give it a rest, Kevin. We'll be out of here before you know it."

Ben ran up to the front door and rang the bell. The door was opened by a chubby boy with blond hair and a pimply face. He was wearing a T-shirt that said "Geeks Rule."

"Hey, Cooper!" Ben said. "Happy birthday."

"It's great to see you guys," Cooper said, smiling. "Come on inside."

They followed Cooper inside to the living room. Clear plastic covered the flowery couch and loveseat.

"So where is everybody?" Ben asked.

"You're here!" Cooper replied cheerfully. "Let's get this party started!"

"Oh, great," Kevin moaned. "You mean nobody else is coming?"

"Well, I invited my grandma, but it's Bingo night," Cooper explained. "We don't need anybody else, anyway. This is going to be an awesome party. My mom even ordered a pizza."

Cooper motioned to a pizza box on the coffee table. Kevin flipped open the lid.

"There's only one slice in there," he said.

Cooper blushed. "Well, I might have eaten some of it while I was waiting for you guys. You're late."

"Actually, we're five minutes early," Gwen chimed in.

Cooper sidled up to Gwen. "That's really sweet of you to come early. It means a lot to me."

Gwen sighed. Cooper had had a crush on her since they were both kids.

"Actually, my watch is just slow," she said.

Ben thrust a present into Cooper's hands. "Here, we got you something."

"Hey, cool!" he said, tearing off the paper. "A Captain Outrageous action figure! Just what I wanted!"

"We know," Gwen said dryly, "you told us."

Cooper raced out of the living room. Ben looked at the others and shrugged. Then they followed him down the hallway into Cooper's bedroom.

Shelves lined three walls of Cooper's room from corner to corner. The shelves were filled with what looked like every action figure ever made. The fourth wall contained Cooper's amazing computer setup. He had three monitors and five blinking hard drives. Ship jumped out of Julie's arms and began sniffing around with excitement.

Kevin pointed to a Captain Outrageous action figure sitting on top of one of the drives.

"Hey, you already have that," he said.

"I had *one*," Cooper corrected him. "Everyone knows you need two of each action figure. One to keep in the box, and one to take out and play with."

"That's it, I'm outta here," Kevin said. "I'm too old to play with toys."

Cooper ran to the door and blocked it with his body. "Don't go! Forget about Captain Outrageous. Check out this wicked alien tech I just scored."

That was enough to stop Kevin. Trading in alien technology was a hobby of his, and one that had gotten him into trouble more than once. But Kevin was fascinated by each new device he came across. Each one was more surprising than the last.

"Check this out," Cooper said. He pushed aside a pile of clothes to reveal a black cube with strange markings on it. Kevin's eyes widened.

"Is that what I think it is?" he asked.

Cooper nodded. "It's a Narvian transporter. I haven't figured out exactly how it works yet, but I'm close."

Kevin whistled. "That is some serious tech, dude. You'd better be careful with that. Maybe I should check it out for you."

Cooper quickly covered it again, grinning. He was happy to have something to lord over Kevin for once. "No thanks. I've got it." He nodded over to his computer station. "I've got something else to show you. Check this out."

Cooper sat at his desk and started typing into his keyboard. A starry scene popped up on the largest computer screen. Cooper zoomed in on a picture of two planets, a small brown one and a larger white one.

"I hacked into this intergalactic role-playing game," Cooper said. "It's way better than any game on Earth. I haven't been able to translate the alien writing, but I pretty much got it figured out. You pick a planet, and then use its weapons system to attack other planets. I'm the small brown planet. I call it 'Planet Cooper.' I launched a totally sick attack on that white planet there, Planet Kevin."

"Hey!" Kevin protested.

"It's just a game," Cooper said. "I don't know the real name, but I like to call it 'Galaxy Wars.' You should try it."

Cooper started typing on the keyboard, and a weapons schematic appeared on the screen. The diagram was labeled with alien writing.

"That looks familiar," Kevin said thoughtfully.

"Yeah, whatever," Cooper said. His eyes glazed over as he played the game.

"Uh, Cooper, could we do something else?" Ben asked.

"Sure," Cooper said. He handed Ben a remote. "Why don't you turn on that TV over there?"

Ben sighed and switched on the television set. He pushed some clothes off of Cooper's bed and sat down. Julie, Kevin, and Gwen glared at him.

"Might as well make ourselves comfortable," he said.

The face of a newscaster appeared on the TV screen. She was holding a microphone and standing in front of the center of town in Bellwood. Behind her, people were running and screaming.

"Uh oh," Gwen said. "This doesn't look good."

"Downtown Bellwood is under attack from an alien creature in a spaceship!" the newscaster announced. "Could this be one of the many forms of that menace, Ben Tennyson?"

Ben jumped up. "Sorry, Coop," he said. "Gotta run!"

Ben raced through the back streets of Bellwood, taking a shortcut downtown. His green souped-up muscle car was loaded with alien tech — and a killer engine.

"It's so unfair that the media keeps blaming everything on you," Julie said from the passenger seat. "You're the one saving everybody when aliens attack."

Kevin stuck his head between them. "It's not like he does it alone," he said. "Gwen and I have saved his butt more than once, you know."

"That's true," Julie agreed. "But at least you guys haven't been labeled Public Enemy Number One."

"It's not so bad," Ben said. Then he turned a corner, driving right into a crowd of protesters carrying signs.

"Keep Aliens Out of Bellwood!"

"Send Ben Back to Outer Space!"

"Ban Ben!"

"Okay, maybe it is," Ben admitted.

Anyone looking at Ben would find it hard to believe he was considered a threat to Bellwood. He was a clean-cut looking kid with short brown hair. But ever since an eager fan had revealed his secret on the web, Ben had experienced nothing but trouble.

It wasn't like he'd ever asked to be able to turn into aliens. Ben didn't know what the Omnitrix was when he discovered it and put it on his wrist—and he certainly didn't know it was nearly impossible to take off. He was ten years old back then, and the Omnitrix allowed him to transform into ten different aliens. He proudly wore the number 10 on his green jacket in honor of those first years.

The Omnitrix introduced more alien forms as Ben grew older. Ben thought it was the most powerful thing in the universe—until the Omnitrix got an upgrade. Now Ben wore the Ultrimatrix on his wrist. He still wasn't sure of everything it was capable of. He only knew that like the Omnitrix, the Ultrimatrix device contained the genetic code for countless life-forms found all over the universe. Ben just had to activate it, and *bam!* He transformed instantly.

Ben steered the car to the curb and made his way through the crowd, followed by Kevin, Gwen, and Julie. Nobody even noticed Ben in his human form. All eyes were on the spaceship that was busy decimating downtown.

The donut-shaped ship wasn't much bigger than an SUV. A clear domed bubble rose up from the center of the donut. Ben could see the pilot, an alien with a furry face and a twitching black nose. He looked panicked, and he seemed to have lost control of his ship. It dove low over the heads of the crowd, then picked up again and flew right through a billboard advertising Crystal Cola.

"Is that a spaceship or a car from an amusement park ride?" Kevin asked.

"I don't know, but whatever it is, it's not from around here," Ben replied.

The ship veered up sharply, flying over the trees that lined the once-peaceful street. Leaves went flying in all directions as the alien ship sheared them right off.

A frightened man ran past them. "Somebody stop Ben Tennyson before he destroys us all!"

Ben sighed. "Really? Do they think I'm that lame?"

He held up his wrist and activated an alien form on his Ultrimatrix. "Let's go Diamondhead!" Ben cried. He punched a button on the Ultrimatrix and a bright green light washed over his body. When the light faded, an alien stood in Ben's place. Diamondhead's powerful body was made of a substance harder than diamond. Sharp crystalline points grew from his back, and he wore a sleeveless one-piece outfit that was black on the right side, and white on the left side. His hard-muscled upper arms looked like boulders, and his hands were hard-hitting hammers.

"I'll stabilize him for you," Gwen offered. Her grandmother was an Anodite alien, and Gwen had inherited several unique abilities from her. She raised both hands in the air, palms out, and waves of pink energy poured out from them. The pink energy formed a bubble around the ship just as it ricocheted off of a two-story office building, sending bricks and debris tumbling down below.

Gwen strained to hold the ship inside the bubble. She slowly lowered her hands, and the spaceship hovered a few feet above the street.

"My turn," Diamondhead said in a deep voice. The bubble evaporated, and Diamondhead's massive fist came crashing down on the front of the ship. The metal dented, but it didn't cripple the ship like Diamondhead had hoped. Whatever that metal was, it was tough stuff.

Inside, the alien pilot looked terrified. With a loud cry, Diamondhead picked up the ship and pounded it on the street. The pavement cracked, but the spaceship remained unharmed.

Frustrated now, Diamondhead raised both arms in the air.

BAM! He brought them both down on the clear hood covering the pilot, shattering it. The pilot covered his head with his hands.

"Please, please, don't hurt me!" the alien begged.

Kevin ran up and grabbed the controls from the pilot. He pulled some levers and pressed some buttons, and the ship lost power. Diamondhead pulled the alien out of his seat. He was about the size of a five-year-old Earth child.

"What brings you to Bellwood?" Diamondhead asked.

"I come in peace!" the alien yelled. "I am not here to attack. I am looking for someone called Ben Tennyson. My planet needs his help!"

Diamondhead set the alien on the ground. Green light flashed over his body, and Ben returned to his human form.

"You know, I really should start giving out my cell phone number," Ben said. "Things would be so much easier!"

Well, what do you know?" Grandpa Max exclaimed in surprise. "You're a Pratarian, right?"

Ben and Gwen's grandfather wheeled his chair out from behind his computer station. He spent most of his time in the Plumbers Comm Center, monitoring the universe for signs of illegal intergalactic activity. Ben, Gwen, and Julie left downtown and took the alien straight to Grandpa Max, while Kevin took care of towing the alien's spaceship.

"Yes, I am a Cynomydan from the planet Prataria," the alien replied. "My name is Invul."

"Nice to meet you, Invul," Grandpa Max said. He clasped Invul's furry hand in his own and shook his arm up and down. "What brings you to Earth? I heard you caused a bit of a commotion downtown."

"That's an understatement," Gwen said. "He practically leveled Main Street, and, as usual, everyone's blaming Ben."

"The Ultrimatrix contains great power, and with great power comes great responsibility," Grandpa Max said. "Ben's just going to have to learn how to handle it."

"Gee, thanks for the warm and fuzzy sympathy, Gramps," Ben said. "Anyway, we got him here in one piece. His says his planet needs my help."

"I apologize for the destruction I caused, but my navigation systems were damaged when I entered your Earth's atmosphere," Invul explained. His nose twitched nervously as he talked. Ben thought he looked like a cross between a humanoid and some kind of rodent—a cute one, like a prairie dog, maybe. He wore a brown jumpsuit with a dark brown circle sewn onto the front pocket. "What the great Ben Tennyson says is true. The people of my planet need your assistance. I am an ambassador of Prataria, sent here with this plea for help."

"I took a jaunt to Prataria once when I was younger," Grandpa Max said. "That underground society of yours is pretty amazing. And your defense system is one of the best I've ever encountered."

Invul nodded. "Ages ago, our planet was attacked by another planet," he explained. "The weapons they used contained high levels of radiation, decimating all life on the planet's surface. The Cynomydan species was one of the few to survive. We were able to thrive underground, and rebuilt our society over thousands of years."

"That would explain the excellent defense system," Gwen guessed. "After what you went through, you'd want to protect the planet from another devastating attack."

"Exactly," Invul said. "But now we are under attack again, and we are not sure if our defense system can withstand what the Hedillans have in store. We believe they have a weapon capable of decimating any defense system."

Grandpa Max gave a low whistle. "The Hedillans? Those guys are master weapons manufacturers. Generally, though, they prefer to make money selling weapons, rather than use them. Do you know why they would attack you?"

"Because we attacked them first," Invul replied.

"Um, that doesn't sound like such a smart move," Kevin said. "Why would you do that?"

"But we *didn't*," Invul said. "That's the problem. Our weapons system activated independently, attacking the comm center in orbit around the planet Ventulus."

"You mean your weapons system was hacked?" Ben asked.

"We don't know," Invul said. "Our scientists investigated, and there doesn't seem to be a malfunction in the system of any kind. The most likely answer is that someone has somehow taken control of our weapons systems and attacked Ventulus. We just don't know why. That's why I came here to find you. We need your help. Ventulus has declared war on us."

Kevin came into the office, holding a chunk of metal in his hands. "Your ship's in the garage, but it's pretty messed up," he said. "Although I gotta say it's pretty impressive for something that looks like you'd put a quarter in to ride at the supermarket. This metal's some of the strongest I've ever seen."

Invul smiled proudly. "That's Inextrium," he said. "My people have been mining it for years. It's practically indestructible."

Ben rubbed his hand, remembering how hard Diamondhead had hit the hull. "Yeah, I know."

Kevin tossed the chunk of metal in the air. "If you don't mind, I'd like to hang on to this. It could come in handy." He gripped the metal, and his hand and forearm absorbed it, turning a shade of dull silver. "Indestructible hand. Cool."

"You are welcome to it," Invul said. "I am grateful for your help."

"Honestly, I'm not sure how we can help you," Ben said. "Do you have any idea who's hacking your system?"

Invul shook his head. "None at all." He nodded toward Max's computer. "May I?"

"Be my guest," Max said.

Invul walked up to the keyboard. He was so short his hands could barely reach it, but that didn't stop him from furiously typing on it. A weapons system schematic popped up on the screen. Strange alien writing was scrawled all over the diagram.

"That looks familiar," Julie said.

Ben, Gwen, and Kevin looked at each other. "Cooper!" they cried at once.

CHAPTER FOUR

Hey, you're twisting my arm!" Cooper yelled.

Kevin ushered Cooper into Grandpa Max's office, dragging him by the elbow. It had only taken him ten minutes to race to Cooper's house and bring him back to Plumbers HQ. Kevin pushed Cooper down on a seat in front of Max's computer station.

"Look familiar to you?" Kevin asked, pointing to the Pratarian weapons schematic.

"Sure," Cooper replied. "That's the weapons system for Planet Cooper."

Invul stepped forward. "I do not understand," he said. "What is this Planet Cooper?"

Cooper wheeled his chair backward in alarm. "Whoa! Who's the talking furball?"

"He's from the planet Prataria," Ben answered. "It's a *real* planet, not some planet in a fake role-playing game."

Cooper looked confused.

"You hacked into a real planet's weapons system, genius," Kevin explained. "While you were having fun, you started a war."

"Cool!" Cooper said, then quickly regretted it. "I mean, you have to admit the whole thing's pretty amazing. I thought I was hacking into a game. I never meant to start a real war."

Invul looked shocked. "This . . . this stringy-haired Earthling is the reason our planet is in peril?"

"Hey, at least I'm not covered in fur," Cooper protested.

"Cooper!" Gwen snapped. "You've really messed up here. Now you've got to make it right."

Cooper wheeled up to the keyboard. "No problem. I'll just blast Planet Kevin—or whatever the real planet is called—and the whole war will end with a bang."

"The planet is called Ventulus," Invul said. "And that solution is *not* acceptable. We Pratarians are a peace-loving people. We will not condone the destruction of another planet, especially because of some stupid mistake."

"It was pretty brilliant, actually," Cooper said. "Do you know how hard it is to hack your systems?"

"Maybe we can just explain to the Hedillans what happened," Ben suggested. "Cooper, can you get visual communication going with their military leaders?"

"You bet," Cooper replied.

Grandpa Max thoughtfully stroked his chin. "The Hedillans can get pretty nasty when they're provoked," he said. "I'm not sure if that's such a good idea."

"The worst they can say is no, right?" Ben asked. "It's worth a try. Invul, maybe you should start the conversation."

Invul looked terrified. "Me?"

"They'll need to know that the Pratarians are aware of what Cooper is doing," Ben said. "Don't worry, we'll be right behind you."

"Got it!" Cooper called out.

An image of an alien with huge black eyes, a pure white face with a small mouth, and two antennae filled the screen.

"This is General Stratus of the Hedillan army," said the

alien. "How did you break into this comm channel?"

Invul stepped in front of the screen, his nose twitching nervously. "I am Invul, an ambassador from the planet Prataria," he said. "General, the attack on Ventulus was a huge mistake. An Earthling hacked into our weapons system and initiated the attack. The Pratarians want nothing but peace with your planet."

"Preposterous!" General Stratus boomed. "Your attack was a foolish act of misguided bravery. Now that you realize that you cannot defeat our technology, you're scurrying back into your holes like cowards."

"No, General, it's true!" Invul cried.

Ben stepped beside Invul. "He's not lying, sir. We have the hacker right here. He can explain how he did it."

General Stratus's antennae twisted violently. "I know that face! Ben Tennyson, wielder of the Ultrimatrix, one of the most powerful weapons in the universe. So you have allied with the Pratarians, have you?"

"No, that's not what this is about!" Ben protested.

"Monarch will be pleased with my report," General Stratus replied. "Right now, we are gearing up *our* most powerful weapon. The Pratarian defense systems cannot withstand it. Not even *you* can withstand it, Ben Tennyson."

Invul looked like he might faint.

"General, you're making a huge mistake!" Ben cried.

General Stratus grinned. "No, the Pratarians made a huge mistake when they attacked us," he said. "And soon you will pay. We will annihilate Prataria!"

CHAPTER FIVE

The screen went blank.

"Well, at least we tried," Cooper said, shrugging.

"Oh dear, oh dear!" Invul moaned. "Our planet is doomed!"

"There's still time," Ben said. "I think we can still reason with the Hedillans. Julie, can we use Ship to travel to Ventulus?"

"Sure," Julie said, "as long as I can come, too."

"I'm not so sure about this, Ben," Grandpa Max warned. "The Hedillans might live in the clouds, but they're as stubborn as rocks."

"We still have to try," Ben replied. "We can't just let them sit back and destroy Prataria."

"Maybe Cooper's idea to blast Ventulus first wasn't so bad," Kevin said. "I mean, if they won't back down, why not?"

Cooper's blue eyes widened. "You're actually agreeing with me?"

"No, he's not," Gwen said firmly. "Cooper, you should use your talents to try to stop the attack, not start another one. Stay here and try to hack into the Hedillans' weapons system and stop that mega-weapon the general was talking about."

"That'll be a snap," Cooper bragged. He wiggled his eyebrows at Gwen. "Although, I could use a lovely assistant. Maybe you should stay back and help me."

"I'm sure you'll do just fine by yourself, Cooper," Gwen told him in a voice as smooth as butter.

"And I'll keep an eye on him to make sure he doesn't do anything stupid," Grandpa Max growled.

"Too late for that," Kevin said dryly. "Come on. Let's power up Ship."

Julie picked up Ship. "Do you mind helping us out, Ship?" she asked.

Ship made a happy noise and wagged his "tail" to show he was excited.

"Okay," she told the others. "I guess we'd better do this outside."

"Before we go, I must contact my leader," Invul said. He took a communicator from his pocket and activated it. "Sir, Ambassador Invul here. I have found Ben Tennyson."

Ben looked over Invul's shoulder and saw the face in the communicator. Like Invul, the alien had a furry face and black nose. But the fur on his chin was white and bushy, like a beard.

"Excellent!" said the Pratarian leader. "Can he help solve our problem?"

"We are trying, To-Nel," Invul said. "It seems that the commandeering of our weapons system was an accident, of sorts. I tried to explain that to the Hedillans, but they won't listen. They have threatened to destroy Prataria."

To-Nel frowned. "Then the fate we have worked so hard to prevent is upon us."

"There is still hope," Invul said. "Ben Tennyson and his friends are traveling with me to Ventulus to reason with the Hedillan leader in person."

A dark cloud crossed To-Nel's face. "I wish you luck, Invul. But I fear the Hedillans are beyond reason."

Invul ended the communication with a sigh. "I hope he is wrong!"

They left Cooper and Grandpa Max in the office and walked upstairs, out of the auto shop, and into the lot out back.

"Ship, we need a Galvani Gunship, please," Ben said.

Ship ran away from them to the center of the lot. He wagged his tail once more.

Then his tiny body began to grow and expand, forming shapes—platforms, control panels, walls, and wings. The entire spaceship unfolded right before their eyes.

The main door swung down, and Ben and the others climbed inside and entered the bridge. The entire ship was black and neon green, just like Ship, but otherwise it was an exact duplicate of a Galvani Gunship, complete with shields and laser cannons tucked under the wings. Invul looked around nervously.

Kevin sat in the pilot's seat. "I love driving this baby," he said.

Ben raced up behind him, seconds too late to take the seat. "Aw, man! You got to drive last time!"

"It's rather large, isn't it?" Invul asked. "How does it manage long-distance travel?"

"It's loaded with a couple of sweet warp engines," Kevin replied. "Fastest in the galaxy."

"Our ships are designed to travel through wormholes," Invul said. "Our astronomers have spent years mapping the wormholes in this part of the galaxy and determining their destinations. It's not always an accurate method, but we don't do much space traveling anyway. I'm the first ambassador to leave the planet in nearly 20 years."

"We'd better take off," Ben said. "The quicker we get to Ventulus, the sooner we can stop them from destroying Prataria."

"I need to know where we're going first," Kevin said. "Invul, can you give me some coordinates?"

"Certainly," Invul replied. He approached Kevin and the two of them quickly programmed the ship for Ventulus space. Then Ben, Julie, Gwen, and Invul strapped themselves to their seats.

"All right, Ship!" Kevin said. "Let's go!"

Ship gracefully floated off the ground and then quickly zoomed across the sky, traveling faster and faster through Earth's atmosphere. Within moments they were in the planet's orbit, a small craft in a sea of star-studded blackness.

"Time to kick it," Kevin said, pressing the button for the warp engines. "Hold on, everybody!"

Ben's stomach lurched as Ship switched to warp drive, racing through the galaxy faster than the speed of light. He'd done it before, and he knew he would get used to the sensation soon. Outside the window, the black sky was now streaked with the blurry white light of stars as they sped by.

Kevin switched on the automatic pilot and swung around in his seat to face the others.

"So," he said. "Once we get to Ventulus, what's the plan?"

"I'm thinking we can use Ship's cloaking device to dock in a transport bay in the capital city," Ben said. "Once we're safely in, we can talk to the Hedillan leader."

"Or get dragged off to Hedillan prison," Gwen said thoughtfully. "Is that really the only way?"

"We could try announcing our approach, but something tells me we'd be blasted out of the sky before we had a chance to explain," Ben replied.

"I am afraid he is right," Invul said. "The cloaking device may be our best chance." He gazed out the window and tightly gripped the arms of his seat. "I hope we get there soon. Being out in open space like this is very taxing. I feel much more comfortable inside a wormhole."

"Your wish is my command," Kevin replied, pulling a lever on the controls. The warp engines quieted down as Ship floated to a stop in space. "We're entering Ventulus space now."

"Ship, activate cloaking device," Ben called out. "Then proceed to the nearest transport bay you can find."

Ship beeped in reply and a glowing shield appeared around the craft, capable of blocking Ship's presence both visually and on radar. Kevin carefully steered toward the transport bay, a busy hub. Several Hedillan ships were also moving toward the bay. The graceful white ships looked like the Hedillans themselves: bright white with one round wing on each side. Two bulbous windows in the front of each ship were shaped like the Hedillan's large, round eyes.

"Careful, Kevin," Gwen warned. "Remember, they can't see us. We don't want anybody bumping into us."

"Remember who you're talking to," Kevin told her. "I've got this under control."

Beep! Beep! Beep! Beep! Beep!

An alarm sounded as green lights flashed a warning inside the cabin.

"The cloaking device is down!" Kevin cried, frantically trying to raise the shield again.

"Under control, huh?" Gwen muttered.

The Hedillan ships flew out of their neat formation and completely surrounded Ship. General Stratus's face appeared on the control screen.

"Ben Tennyson. I should have known," he said. "Your attempt to attack our planet has been thwarted. Surrender immediately!"

CHAPTER SIX

We're not here to attack," Ben said. He ran to the pilot's seat and leaned over Kevin's shoulder. "See? We're shutting down our weapons."

"We're what?!" Kevin cried.

"You have no choice," General Stratus informed them. "If you do not, your ship will be destroyed immediately. Follow our ships into the transport bay and prepare to surrender to our leader."

The screen went black.

"He doesn't seem very friendly," Julie remarked. "I hope he doesn't do anything to hurt Ship."

"What do you say, cuz?" Gwen asked. "Ship's got more power than they realize. We could break through this blockade right now without getting hurt and be back to Earth before bedtime."

Ben shook his head. "If we do that, there's no hope for Prataria," he said. "This is no big deal, really. We were going to try to get to the Hedillan leader anyway. This just makes it easier."

"No big deal, huh?" Kevin asked. "That's easy to say when you've got an alien army strapped to your wrist."

"This is just dreadful!" Invul exclaimed. "I am so sorry to get you all mixed up in this."

"Our friend is the one who started the trouble," Ben reminded him. "But we'd help you anyway. Don't worry, it's going to be fine."

They followed the Hedillan ships into the transport bay. General Stratus appeared onscreen again once they docked.

"Remove all weapons, put your hands in the air, and exit your craft," he ordered.

"No problem!" Ben said cheerfully. "Ship, open up!"

Ship obeyed, and Ben walked down the gangway followed by Invul, Julie, Gwen, and a very wary-looking Kevin. Julie patted Ship as she left.

"Stay right here, Ship," she said quietly. "We'll be back to get you, I promise."

Then a small regiment of Hedillan soldiers descended on them, each one brandishing a sleek white weapon. General Stratus marched through them and stood face to face with Ben.

"How foolish of you to think a cloaking device could get past our detectors," he said. "I will enjoy seeing what Monarch has planned for you."

"Monarch's just the guy we want to see," Ben told him.

As the soldiers marched them through a series of hallways, Ben got a glimpse of the capital city through the windows. All of the buildings were shaped like circles, and each one was supported by a pole that seemed too impossibly thin to support the giant building on top. Ben looked down but couldn't see the planet's surface at all; thin, wispy clouds floated all around them. The Hedillans obviously preferred living in the sky.

They arrived in a large round chamber with a circular white table in the center. Hedillans in pale blue robes sat around a table and one of them rose when they entered.

"Good work, General Stratus," Monarch said. "You are a credit to Ventulus."

General Stratus bowed his head. "Thank you, Monarch."

Monarch approached them, pausing to stop in front of Invul. He looked down at him with a slight sneer on his face.

"What have we here? A Pratarian in the Hedillan high chambers?" he asked. "You've come a long way from your hole in the ground, haven't you?"

"I come with a message of peace," Invul said, refusing to respond to the taunt. "Our people did not attack you. An Earthling hacked into our weapons system and attacked you, thinking he was playing some kind of game."

Monarch's eyes swiftly turned to observe Ben, Gwen, Kevin, and Julie. "One of these humans?"

Ben stepped forward. "No, but he's a friend of ours. He's smart about some things, but really stupid about others," he said. "We came here to explain everything to you. Please call off your plans to destroy Prataria."

"Don't listen to him, sir!" General Stratus called out. "Their ship was armed, and they entered Ventulus space heavily cloaked."

"If we hadn't been cloaked we never would have been able to dock in your city and talk to you," Ben said. "Besides, if we were here to attack, how much damage could we really do with one Pratarian, a few young humans, and one ship?"

Monarch looked thoughtful. But Stratus was still suspicious.

"They could be scouts, charged with reporting back to their army," the general proposed. "I do not trust them, especially their leader, Ben Tennyson. He is known for interfering on many planets throughout the universe."

"I too have read the reports," Monarch said. "And if I recall, Ben Tennyson's interference involves preventing conflicts, not causing them."

"That's right!" Julie said bravely.

Monarch bowed his head. "In an act of trust and good will, I will set you free. You may—"

BOOM!

A huge explosion shook the chamber with a jolt so powerful it knocked everyone off of their feet. Ben slammed into Invul with a thud. The two of them rolled right in front of Monarch.

"It's an attack!" General Stratus yelled.

The comm screen on the wall flashed on, and To-Nel's bearded face appeared.

"This is a warning to the Hedillans," he announced. "The Pratarians have always been a peaceful people. But our peaceful ways nearly led to our extinction years ago.

We will not sit back and allow our planet to be destroyed. This time, we are fighting back!"

"To-Nel, no!" Invul cried. "Our mission was successful. Monarch was just about to call off the attack on Prataria."

"You are trusting, Invul," he said. "Too trusting. I have conferred with the Pratarian council, and it has been decided. We will fight!"

The screen flashed off. General Stratus pointed a long, thin finger at Ben.

"I told you! They are spies!" he yelled.

"It would appear that you are right, general," Monarch agreed. "Take them to the prison!"

CHAPTER SEVEN

The Hedillan soldiers jumped to their feet and began to converge on Ben and the others. At the same time, a black and neon-green hover scooter flew into the room.

"Ship!" Julie cried. She quickly jumped on his back.

Ben activated an alien on the Ultrimatrix. The green light from the device blinded the Hedillans for a minute, giving Ben and the others a chance to make a break. Gwen immediately threw up a field of pink energy between her and the soldiers. She, Kevin, and Julie were on one side of the shield, but Ben and Invul were on the other side, across the room.

"Go Spidermonkey!" Ben cried, as he transformed into a blue monkeylike alien with four arms, four eyes, and a long tail. He grabbed Invul with one of his arms and jumped up, grabbing a light hanging down from the ceiling.

Four Hedillans reached for Invul at once, pulling him out of Spidermonkey's grasp.

"Invul, no!" Spidermonkey yelled.

He swung back to try to grab Invul again, but two Hedillan soldiers ran up to him from both sides. Spidermonkey had no choice. He sailed over their heads and followed Gwen, Kevin, and Julie out of the chamber.

An alarm rang through the building as they ran through the long passageway to the transport bay. A sleek metal door slid down from the ceiling, blocking their path. Spidermonkey jumped down to the ground.

"I got this one," Kevin said. He took the piece of Pratarian metal from his pocket and absorbed it with his right fist and lower arm.

Bam! He punched right through the door.

"Nice!" Spidermonkey said.

"They're going to have the transport bay on lockdown," Gwen remarked. She was running backward, keeping the pink energy shields behind them. "We won't be able to escape."

Ship, in his form as a hover scooter, started beeping.

"I think Ship has an idea," Julie said.

"All right," Ben said. "Let's follow Ship!"

Kevin punched his way through two more metal doors as they ran. Ship suddenly came to a stop in front of what looked like a ventilation shaft.

Kevin ripped the grid off of the shaft. "Let's go," he said. "I'll go last and replace the cover. If we're quick, they won't realize where we've gone."

One by one they slid down the shaft. Ship had led them into a small storage locker at the base of the city. Ben transformed back into a human.

"Good thinking, Ship," he said. "It'll be a few minutes before they find us here. We can come up with a plan."

"I say we blast our way out of here," Kevin suggested. "Ship's weapons are powerful enough to do it."

"But we can't leave Invul behind," Ben reminded him. "Not to mention that things are worse than ever. Thanks to Cooper, both planets are likely to end up in pieces."

"Speaking of Cooper, I wonder if he's been able to deactivate the Hedillans' mega-weapon," Gwen said. She took a cell phone from her pocket.

"Um, I don't think you get service here," Kevin joked.

"Grandpa souped up my cell for me. No dead zones, no matter where you are in the universe," Gwen said.

She dialed up Cooper. His face lit up on the small video screen when he saw Gwen was calling.

"Gwen! Did you miss me?" he asked.

Gwen ignored him. "How's it going with the mega-weapon?" she asked.

Cooper frowned. "Not good. I figured out how to deactivate it, but it can't be done remotely. It has to be done in person."

"Then let's trash the thing and then get out of here," Kevin suggested.

Ben leaned over Gwen's shoulder. "Cooper, is it located in the capital city?"

Cooper nodded. "In the building you're standing in, as a matter of fact. I can give you the coordinates."

A plan quickly formed in Ben's mind.

"Gwen, I need you to help me find Invul. You can track his signal. Kevin, take the communicator and let

Cooper show you how to deactivate the mega-weapon."
He turned to Julie.

"Do you think you and Ship can get to the transport bay?" he asked.

Julie nodded. "Sure."

"Then have Ship transform into a Hedillan ship and wait there for us. You should be safe. Once we've done what we've got to do we'll meet you in the bay," Ben told her.

"Sounds like a plan!" Kevin said.

CHAPTER EiGHT

In order for this to work, you have to do everything I say," Cooper told Kevin through Gwen's cell phone.

"How did I get this assignment again?" Kevin muttered.

They had managed to leave the storage locker without being detected. Julie and Ship headed to the transport center. Gwen used her psychic abilities to put a lock on Invul's energy, and she and Ben made their way through the Hedillan prison.

Kevin climbed up a narrow spiral staircase.

"The mega-weapon is located on the top level of the city," Cooper explained. "You'll have to pass through three security doors to get to it, but I can get those open for you. The first one should be about twenty steps up."

Kevin made his way up the staircase and just as Cooper had said, there was a small landing in front of a security door. Lights flashed on a keypad next to the door.

"All right, I'm here," Kevin reported.

"Give me a sec," Cooper said.

The lights on the keypad stopped flashing, and the security door slid open.

"From what I can tell they store their secondary weapons here," Cooper said as Kevin stepped through the door. "Although you should be careful when you enter. It's probably guarded by—"

"Hedillan soldiers," Kevin finished for him. Four Hedillans with laser guns spun around and lifted their weapons, pointing toward Kevin.

Kevin had to think fast. The chunk of Pratarian metal in his arm was too small to turn his whole body into metal. He needed something bigger. He whirled around and absorbed the first thing within reach—a strange silver globe resting on a pedestal.

His whole body turned the same color as the metal. He had no idea how strong it was—but something didn't feel right.

The laser guns began to wobble in the hands of the soldiers. They flew toward Kevin, attaching to his arms and legs!

"Guess I'm magnetic," Kevin realized. "Could be worse."

The Hedillan soldiers were confused for a moment. Kevin took advantage and lunged at them, slamming each one with a powerful metal punch. The soldiers slumped to the floor.

Kevin switched on the cell phone. "I took care of them," he told Cooper. "What next?"

"Head to the far wall and—" Cooper's instructions were interrupted by a cry from Kevin. A strong magnetic pull was dragging him toward a huge missile located in the center of the room. Kevin tried to break away, but the pull was too strong. There was a loud clang of metal on metal as Kevin slammed into the missile.

One of the downed Hedillan soldiers crawled to his feet. He pulled himself over to a control panel. Kevin kicked at him with his free foot, but the soldier activated the missile before Kevin's foot made contact and the Hedillan collapsed once more. Kevin heard a sound overhead and looked up to see the domed ceiling sliding open. The missile was about to launch!

Kevin tried to change back to his normal form, but couldn't.

"What's going on?" Cooper asked.

"I'm kinda stuck right now," Kevin said. "Cooper, any chance you can stop the missile in here from firing? I've got this magnetic thing going on and I can't break away or turn back."

"Let me see," Cooper said.

"Hurry up, will you?" Kevin asked.

An alien symbol flashed on the missile control panel. Then a different symbol flashed a second later. Kevin knew what it was—a countdown!

"Any time now, Cooper," Kevin said.

"All right! All right!" Cooper cried.

Kevin watched the digits on the screen, counting in his head. *Six . . . five . . . four . . . three . . . two . . .*

The control panel blinked off. Kevin slid off of the missile onto the floor.

"Did it work?" Cooper asked. "I flooded the missile with a negative charge to break up the magnetic energy. You should be able to change back now."

Kevin morphed back into human form.

"Thanks, Cooper," he said grudgingly. "All right, dude. What's next?"

CHAPTER NINE

I don't think Invul's in this building anymore," Gwen said, pressing her fingers to her forehead.

Ben and Gwen cautiously made their way through the building, traveling in the air vents on hands and knees. So far, they had managed to avoid the Hedillans.

"Did you lose him?" Ben asked.

"Not entirely," Gwen said. "He's close. I think he may be in the next building."

Ben remembered the city, with tall, tree-like buildings that towered high above the surface. "How do the Hedillans get back and forth? I didn't see any roads connecting the buildings," he wondered.

"Maybe it has something to do with those wings on their backs," Gwen suggested.

"Oh yeah," Ben said sheepishly. "Well, that's no problem for us. We just need a way out of here."

They crawled a little further and Ben slid a panel in the vent aside. They were over one of the hallways on the outer circle of the building with windows that looked out over the city. As Ben watched, a Hedillan walked up to one of the windows and pressed a button on a small panel next to it. The window slid open, and the Hedillan flew outside as the door closed behind him.

"Gwen, do you sense anyone else coming?" he asked.

Gwen closed her eyes. "We're okay if we move quickly."

"Gotcha," Ben said. He jumped off of the vent, activating the Ultrimatrix as he fell. "Jet Ray!"

He transformed in mid-air into the red humanoid alien. Yellow, batlike wings were attached to Jet Ray's thin but powerful arms. He whirled around and plucked Gwen out of the vent.

"Here goes nothing!" Jet Ray cried.

He flew at the window, pressing the button in time to soar out into the Hedillan sky. Gwen pointed to a small building several hundred feet below them.

"Down there," she said. "He's pretty freaked out right now, so his signal is loud and clear."

Jet Ray dove down to the building, circling it. Gwen concentrated on Invul's energy, honing in on his exact position.

"Stop!" she cried out.

Jet Ray paused, hovering in front of the window in front of them. "I don't see a button on the outside," he said. "Cover your face!"

Gwen tucked her head inside her arms as Jet Ray flew right through the window, shattering the glass. He wrapped his arms around Gwen to protect her.

Gwen looked at him, raising her right eyebrow. "There might have been an easier way to do that."

"It worked," Jet Ray replied flatly. "Where is he?"

Gwen nodded to the door in front of them. "In there. I'll take care of it."

Gwen stepped up to the door. "Invul, it's me, Gwen. Are you alone?"

"Oh, Gwen, it's so good to hear your voice! Yes, yes, I am alone!"

"Stand back from the door," she warned.

She heard Invul shuffle backward. Then she

concentrated on forming a powerful blast of pink energy, feeling it flow through her fingers.

Bam! The energy hit the door and it slammed wide open. Gwen and Jet Ray ran inside.

Invul seemed startled to see Jet Ray. "Who is this?"

"I can change forms, remember?" Jet Ray asked. "Come on. We need to fly out of here."

They ran out of the prison cell, only to see two lines of Hedillan soldiers running at them from either direction.

"Not again," Jet Ray complained. He tucked Gwen under one arm and Invul under the other. "Let's fly."

BOOM! BOOM! BOOM! Three loud blasts shook the building, sending Jet Ray, Gwen, and Invul flying backward. The Hedillan soldiers all lost their footing.

Then the floor tilted sideways, sending them all flying across the floor.

"The Pratarians are attacking the *base* of the building this time," Gwen shouted.

Ben realized the danger—the Hedillan buildings were designed like trees with narrow trunks. If the trunks came down, the whole building would fall.

"Hang on," he said. He got to his feet and flew out

the window as Jet Ray. Before he hit activated the Ultrimatrix again.

"Humungousaur!"

The alien that landed on the surface of Ventulus wa a huge, dinosaur-like beast with a massive, muscled body and a long tail. Humungousaur watched as a Pratarian missle dove down from the sky and struck the building right at the base.

The support pole was already cracked and weakened from the previous attacks. The entire building began to fall sideways, like a tree that had been chopped above the roots. Humungousaur could hear the screams of the people trapped inside.

"RAWWWWR!" With a mighty cry, he grabbed the pole like a baseball bat. With all his might, he bore the burden of the tremendous weight of the building. Carefully, he lowered it to the ground.

Gwen and Invul ran up to him through the broken window.

"That was pretty amazing," Gwen said.

Bruised and confused Hedillans began to climb out of the windows. They looked around, dazed. Ben guessed many of them had never walked on the surface of their own planet before.

"Where are we? What happened?"

Ben transformed back into his human form. "We'd better find a way to fly back to the other building," he said. "If I use the Ultrimatrix again so soon, it gets wacky."

"Do we have to fly?" Invul asked, nervously tapping his hands together. "It's so nice here on the ground."

Gwen looked up, pointing. "This might be just what we need."

Hedillan rescue workers were arriving on the scene in small flight pods that looked like clear, floating bubbles. They landed the pods on the ground and left them to attend to the Hedillans pouring out of the fallen building.

"Let's run for it," Ben said. He grabbed Invul's hand and they raced toward the nearest empty pod.

One of the Hedillan workers spotted them. "Stop them!"

Fortunately, the rescue workers weren't armed. They jumped inside the pod and Gwen briefly examined the controls.

"It's pretty straightforward," she said. "I can get us to the transport bay. I hope we find Julie and Ship there."

"Don't forget Kevin," Ben reminded her. "I wonder if he's had any luck with the mega-weapon?"

They zoomed off the ground as Pratarian missiles whizzed past them. Gwen expertly dodged them as she steered the pod.

"I hope he has," she said. "If not, we're all in big trouble!"

CHAPTER TEN

The Pratarians' aggressive surprise attack was wreaking havoc with the Hedillans. Fortunately, the chaos allowed Gwen, Ben, and Invul to slip into the transport bay in their rescue pod without being noticed. Gwen landed the pod and the three climbed out, making their way through the bay in a low crawl as Hedillan soldiers sped to their warships to make a counterattack.

"Do you see Julie and Ship?" Gwen asked.

Ben poked his head out from behind a Hedillan ship and gazed around. Ship was easy to spot. He had taken on the form of a winged Hedillan fighter—but he was black and neon-green instead of pure, gleaming white.

The three of them ran to Ship.

"Ship! Open up!" Ben hissed.

Julie smiled in relief when she saw them. "You made it!"

"So did you," Ben said. "But you're a little easy to spot."

"Oh, we got spotted all right," Julie said. "A group of Hedillan soldiers got suspicious. I stayed inside Ship and talked to them through the comm link. I told them this was a new prototype developed by General Stratus. It worked like a charm."

Then Julie frowned. "Where's Kevin?" she asked.

"He's not here yet?" Gwen sounded worried.

Just then the comm system crackled, and Monarch's voice filled the cabin of the ship.

"Attention, people of Ventulus City," he began. "The Pratarians have escalated their unwarranted attack against us. Remain in your homes and stay calm. Our mega-weapon has been activated and will launch in thirty minutes. When it strikes, the planet of Prataria will only be a memory. Long live Ventulus!"

"That is so not good," Gwen said.

Ben took out his cell phone, and Gwen raised an eyebrow. "You're not the only one who gets cool stuff from Grandpa," he said. He quickly punched in a number. "Kevin? You there?"

The sound of laser blasts emitted from the phone, and Ben held it away from his ear. Kevin's voice rose above the fray.

"I'm a little busy right now," Kevin yelled. "I've almost made it to the weapons chamber, but there are a lot of bug-eyed soldiers around. I could use a little help."

"I'll go," Gwen offered. "I can trace his energy."

"Should we go with you?" Julie asked.

Ben shook his head. "No. We've got to find a way to stop this war from both sides." He turned to Invul. "How did the Pratarians attack so quickly? Is there a wormhole connecting your two planets?"

Invul nodded. "It's quite remarkable. It takes only seconds to get here in the proper craft."

"Ship, did you make any contact with Invul's ship back in Bellwood?" Ben asked.

Ship beeped in the affirmative.

"Perfect," Ben said. "We're going to jump out of you, and then you can transform. We need to talk to that To-Nel guy."

Gwen grinned. She loved a challenge. "I bet me and Kevin deactivate that weapon before you convince To-Nel to call off his attack."

Ben grinned back at her. "You're on!"

CHAPTER ELEVEN

Gwen jumped out of Ship first. She closed her eyes and concentrated for a moment.

"Got it!" she cried. Kevin was somewhere up high in the building. "Now I just have to find some way to get there."

She spotted a staircase at the far end of the transport bay and ran for it. She bounded up the stairs, grateful that no one had spotted her.

Another explosion hit the building, and Gwen grabbed onto the railing, keeping her balance. When the dust settled, she raced up the next flight of stairs.

Then she heard a voice behind her. "Stop the human!"

Gwen turned to see two Hedillan soldiers

climbing the stairs behind her. Then she heard a noise above and realized more soldiers were climbing downstairs toward her.

She quickly held her arms out at the sides, palms up. Before the Hedillans could fire their weapons she shot out four powerful blasts of pink energy.

Zap! Zap! Zap! Zap! The soldiers tumbled down the stairs. She jumped over the two soldiers in front of her and ran up to the landing. The security door in front of her was open.

She cautiously entered the missile chamber and spotted four Hedillan soldiers on the floor, unconscious.

Kevin! she realized. She ran to the next security door, which was also open.

A laser blast whizzed past her ear.

"Gwen, watch out!" Kevin called.

Kevin had powered up with some kind of green Hedillan metal. He was fighting off at least a dozen Hedillan soldiers. Their blasts hit him, but bounced right off.

"Nice to see you," Kevin said.

"I came as fast as I could," Gwen replied. She started blasting away at the soldiers with her pink energy. "So where's the mega-weapon?"

"Behind that door," Kevin said, nodding toward the far wall.

"Make a run for it!" Gwen yelled over the laser blasts. "I'll cover you."

Zap! Zap! Zap! Gwen took down the Hedillan soldiers one by one as Kevin raced for the door. Now there were only four left standing. She surrounded the four of them in a pink bubble, levitating them so their heads almost touched the high ceiling.

Then SLAM! Something knocked into Gwen from behind. She fell forward, and the pink energy dissipated.

"Immobilize her!" one of the soldiers yelled.

Gwen felt a sharp jolt, and then her whole body froze. She tried to move, but she couldn't. She couldn't even blink.

Kevin paused by the security door, torn. Should he help Gwen, or stop the doom machine?

The door slid open. "This one's a doozy. You've got three seconds to get through," Cooper said. "Once it closes behind you, no one will able to get through."

Kevin knew what he had to do. If he didn't take the chance to stop the mega-weapon, Gwen would be really angry. He'd been dating her long enough to know that an angry Gwen could be dangerous.

"I'll be back for you!" Kevin yelled. Then he jumped through the doorway, and it shut with a clang behind him.

He entered a room with a dome-shaped ceiling. In the center was a huge crystal sphere. Green lights like jagged lightning streaks illuminated the ball from the inside.

"I'm here," Kevin told Cooper. "What do I do now?"

"You need to locate the power core," Cooper told him. "It's some kind of self-generating power source, and it's not linked to the weapons matrix at all. That's why I can't do it from here. But you'd better hurry. This thing's supposed to go off in less than five minutes."

"What does it look like?" Kevin asked impatiently.

"Check around the base of the weapon," Cooper said. "Max helped me translate some of the Hedillan writing, so we think it's some kind of mineral-based rod."

Kevin walked in a circle about halfway around the doomsday machine when he spotted it—a circular box with one green and one white crystal rod sticking out of the center.

"I think I found it," Kevin said. "There's a green rod and a white rod."

"Hmm," Cooper said. "Let me think. It should be the green one. Try removing it."

Kevin got rid of his metal form and carefully reached out to grab the green rod. As his fingers made contact, a sharp jolt zapped his body. He felt strange, almost liquid, and then realized that he was being absorbed by the crystal sphere! He passed right through its walls and floated inside as the green lights flashed around him.

"Um, Kevin?" Cooper asked. "Better not touch that green rod. The white one is the power rod."

"It's a little too late for that, dude," Kevin said. "I'm stuck inside the mega-weapon now. Is there any way I can get out?"

There was a shuffling sound, and then Grandpa Max appeared inside the phone.

"Kevin, what do you mean you're inside the weapon?" Max asked.

"I mean I'm *inside the weapon*," Kevin repeated. "I just don't see an exit sign."

"There is no way out," Grandpa Max said, his voice heavy. "That green rod was one last security measure. Prataria is going to be destroyed in five minutes!"

"Let me guess," Kevin said. "I'm going to blow up along with it?"

Cooper took the phone back. "Kevin, I'm sorry! I'll find a way to get you out of there, I promise!"

CHAPTER TWELVE

As Gwen raced off to help Kevin, Ben, Julie and Invul got ready for their journey to Prataria.

"Okay, Ship," Ben said. "We need you to transform into a Pratarian spaceship."

Ship beeped and began to quickly shift and morph. In a few seconds, a black and neon-green Pratarian ship stood before them. It looked just like Invul's small donut-shaped ship.

The domed lid to the cockpit swung open.

"We'd better hurry," Ben remarked. "Someone's bound to notice us before long."

The three of them squeezed into the cockpit.

"Hey, your elbow's in my face!" Julie told Ben.

"The ship was designed for Pratarian pilots," Invul said apologetically. "Fortunately, our trip will be short."

Bam! Bam! Bam! Three laser blasts hit the ship.

"I guess we've been noticed," Ben quipped.

"Don't worry," Invul said confidently. "Our defense systems are excellent. I'll get us out of here."

Ben was glad to hear the courage in Invul's voice. He seemed more comfortable inside the Pratarian ship than he had all day.

Invul steered the ship through the crowded transport bay. An alarm sounded, and the doors to the bay began to close in front of them.

"It's going to be tight," Ben warned.

"Pratarians function best in closed spaces," Invul reminded him. "Trust me."

Whoosh! Invul zoomed between the narrow opening, and the doors closed behind them just seconds after they passed through.

But the danger wasn't over yet. Six Hedillan ships flew toward them, trying to block their escape.

"Take the controls for a moment, Ben," Invul said. "I've got to program the coordinates for the wormhole."

Ben obeyed. A Hedillan ship was aimed right toward them. Ben pulled up on the controls and the tiny ship soared over the roof of the other ship.

"Ben, there's trouble behind us!" Julie warned.

Ben craned his neck to see three Hedillan ships right on their tail.

"No warp drive on this thing, huh, Invul?" Ben asked.

"Just one moment," Invul said.

Ben tried to make the small ship move faster, but its pace held. The three Hedillan ships fired blast after blast as they zoomed closer and closer . . .

"Here we are," Invul said, typing on the control panel.

The ship violently lurched to the right and then lunged forward. The sound of the Hedillan laser guns faded into silence as Ship tumbled into the swirling vortex of the wormhole.

"It feels like there are cottonballs inside my head," Julie remarked.

"Me too," Ben agreed.

"The sensation will only last a few moments," Invul said. "We're almost there."

WHOOSH! Invul had barely finished speaking when they shot out of the other end of the wormhole. Ben could see a small brown planet floating below them.

"Wow," he said. "That's pretty amazing."

Invul beamed. "We're very proud of our advances in wormhole technology," he said. "They only rival our defense system. That is why To-Nel's attack is so puzzling to me. I did not think our aggressive weapons were capable of launching an attack on a planet like Ventulus."

"How do we find To-Nel?" Ben asked.

"I can park the ship near the palace entrance," Invul replied. "Ambassadorship has its privileges."

As they neared the planet's surface, Ben was amazed to see how truly flat everything was. There were no buildings, no trees, only patches of scrubby plants adding splashes of green to the brown dirt. Huge holes dotted the landscape.

Invul steered the ship on top of a large hole.

"Ambassador Invul, seeking clearance for landing," Invul said into the comm system.

A metal panel covering the hole slid open, and Invul lowered the craft inside.

"How much longer before the mega-weapon activates?" Ben asked.

Julie looked at her watch. "Three minutes," she replied.

Ben looked worried. "I hate to say it, but I hope Gwen wins this one."

Invul steered the ship through a wide underground tunnel that opened up into a huge underground chamber. To-Nel's palace filled the space, a sprawling one-story structure made of glittering black rock.

Invul parked at the palace entrance and they left Ship. The Mechomorph transformed back into his doglike form. Invul marched up to the palace door.

"Ambassador Invul to see Lord To-Nel," Invul told the palace guard.

The guard stepped aside and let them enter. Invul led them through a maze of hallways until they finally reached To-Nel's command center, a square room filled with humming computer stations and large blinking machines. Pratarians raced around the machines, their noses twitching with nervous excitement.

To-Nel looked surprised to see them. "Invul, what brings you here?"

"You must call off the attack," Invul said. "Monarch has a weapon capable of destroying our planet. It will launch in minutes."

"He will not have a chance to launch it," To-Nel promised. "We are decimating their capital city with our missiles."

"I don't understand, Lord To-Nel," Invul said. "When

did our weapons system become so advanced?"

To-Nel paced the floor. "The High Council has been developing the weapons in secret for years. We have always believed that a strong defense system is not enough. The Hedillans have proven us right."

Ben stepped between them. "This doesn't have to happen," he said. "If you surrender now, you can save your planet as well as Ventulus."

"The Pratarians will never surrender," said To-Nel, his dark eyes glittering. "We would rather be destroyed!"

CHAPTER THIRTEEN

Kevin looked at his watch as the digits ticked down second by second. He knew he shouldn't look at it, but he couldn't help it. His three minutes were almost up.

He pounded against the sphere once more with his Pratarian metal hand, hoping to find a way out. But the sphere didn't even crack.

"Come on!" Kevin yelled. "There's got to be a way out!"

"Kevin, I'm here!"

At first, Kevin thought it must be Gwen. He spun around to see Cooper standing there—at least, he thought it was Cooper. The creature before him had blond hair and a chubby body and face, but his pimply skin was pale purple. Instead of arms, he had two purple tentacles growing from each of his shoulders.

"What happened to you?" Kevin asked.

"No time to explain," Cooper said. "Where's the power rod?"

Kevin pointed. "Over there."

Cooper raced over. Kevin glanced at his watch. Less than twenty seconds left. Cooper reached for the white rod with one of his tentacles, but the appendage just flapped up and down.

"Cooper, come on!" Kevin urged.

"Sorry," Cooper said. "I'm not used to these yet."

He tried again, this time wrapping the end of the tentacle around the rod, gently lifting it up. Kevin fell to the floor with a thud as the green lights vanished and the sphere evaporated around him.

"Ow!" Kevin cried.

"You're welcome," Cooper said. "I saved your life again, and saved Prataria too."

"I guess you did," Kevin admitted. "But we wouldn't be in this mess if you hadn't started the war in the first place!"

"To-Nel, this is madness!" Invul said. "Please listen to us."

"My decision has been made," To-Nel replied.

Ben's cell phone rang. He answered it, relieved to see Kevin's face on the screen.

"Mission accomplished," Kevin told him. "The weapon is destroyed."

"Excellent!" Ben said. "Where's Gwen?"

"She's a little tied up right now," Kevin said. "Cooper and I are going to go get her."

"Cooper?" Ben asked. "What's he doing there?"

"I don't know," Kevin said. "I'll tell you when I find out."

Kevin ended the call, and Ben looked up to see To-Nel's grinning face. "Excellent!" he said. "Now the Hedillans will surely crumble under our assault."

"I fear you have been overcome by madness, my lord," Invul said, wringing his hands.

"Me too," Ben said. "Ship! Pratarian spaceship, please!"

The Pratarians in the chamber gasped as Ship

transformed into one of their spacecrafts in front of their eyes. Ben picked up the small general and jumped inside the cockpit.

"Oh dear, oh dear," Invul fretted, but he jumped inside along with Ben. Julie squeezed in last, and the cockpit dome closed.

"What is the meaning of this?" To-Nel fumed.

"I'm sorry, but I can't let you continue this war," Ben replied. "Invul, will this make it through the hallways?"

"It will be tight, but—"

"I know. Pratarians dig closed spaces. Get us out of here. We need to get back to Ventulus, quickly."

"This is an outrage!" To-Nel yelled. "Release me this instant!"

"I am so sorry, my lord," Invul said.

He steered the ship through the palace hallways. A small army of Pratarians gave chase, but they couldn't reach the speed of the ship. Some of them had weapons, but they were hesitant to use them against their leader.

Invul took Ship back through the wormhole, which spat them out into Ventulus space.

"Get as close to the capital city as you can," Ben

instructed. "I think Lord To-Nel needs to see this."

Invul steered the ship toward the top regions of the city. Three large tube-shaped warships were positioned over the buildings, raining down bombs. Hedillan ships flew around them, but they were like mosquitoes buzzing around a dragon.

Invul gasped. "Those warships bear the symbol of Prataria!"

"They are our finest achievement," To-Nel said proudly.

"I wouldn't be so sure about that," Ben said. "Look at what they're doing."

The air was filled with smoke and debris as the Pratarian assault laid waste to the buildings. Hedillans fled the city in swarms of escape pods, narrowly missing death as their homes crashed beneath them.

For the first time, To-Nel lost the fiery look in his eyes. "Oh dear," he said, sounding very much like Invul.

"This is war, Lord To-Nel," Ben said. "You are wreaking the same devastation on Ventulus that was delivered to your planet long ago. Do you really want the Hedillans to suffer the same fate?"

"What have we done?" To-Nel asked, his voice a whisper.

"You can stop this," Ben said. "Ship, take us to Monarch's chamber."

The Hedillan leader's headquarters were still standing, although the Pratarian missiles had taken large chunks out of the roof. Invul used one of the holes to lower Ship directly into the chamber.

They emerged from the cockpit to see Monarch and General Stratus facing Kevin, Gwen, and some purple creature that looked like Cooper. The three of them had their hands restrained behind them. General Stratus was barking at them furiously.

"What have you done with the power core?" he yelled.

"I told you, I don't know what you're talking about," Kevin answered. He nodded toward Ben. "Maybe we should break this up. Looks like you've got company."

General Stratus whirled around. His antennae stood straight on end when he saw Ben, Julie, and the two Pratarians.

"Seize them!" Stratus shouted.

Ben stepped forward with his hands up. "Hold up. We brought the Pratarian ruler here to meet you guys. You really need to work this out."

Monarch stepped forward. "Lord To-Nel? Why would you come here?"

"I did not come here voluntarily," To-Nel replied, glancing at Ben. "But I am glad that I did. This conflict is out of control. I will ask my forces to withdraw immediately. There must be peace between us. This war should never have begun in the first place."

"Yeah, he's right!" Cooper called out. "It's my fault. You guys shouldn't be mad at each other."

The two leaders looked at Ben. "This creature is the reason for all this trouble?" Monarch asked.

Ben shrugged. "Yeah, I know it's hard to believe."

"Please forgive us," To-Nel said. "We will pay for the reconstruction of your city."

Monarch's antennae twitched. "That would be acceptable," he said. Then he nodded toward Cooper. "And what of this one? How shall he pay?"

"I'll do anything you want!" Cooper blurted out. "I can make sure both of your weapons systems are hacker-proof."

Monarch and To-Nel exchanged glances, then nodded to each other.

"It is agreed," Monarch said.

"Thank you," said To-Nel. "This war is over!"

Invul turned to Ben with tears in his brown eyes. "I can't thank you enough, Ben Tennyson. You have saved us all. I am so glad that I found you."

"Anytime," Ben replied with a grin. "You know where to find me. Just next time, maybe you should stay away from Main Street!"

CHAPTER FOURTEEN

"Any luck yet, Ben?" Cooper asked. "I'm losing control of my tentacles."

One of Cooper's tentacles reached over to Gwen and wrapped around her shoulders.

"Hey, watch it!" Gwen said, pushing it off.

"See what I mean?" Cooper asked innocently.

"I'm sure you can control them just fine," Gwen said, her green eyes blazing. "Ben, hurry up!"

They were back in Max's office in Plumbers HQ. Ben fiddled with the dials of his Ultrimatrix. "I have to figure out what alien form merged with Cooper before I can fix his DNA."

"I told you that Narvian transporter was tricky," Kevin said.

"If I hadn't used that Narvian transporter, you'd be dead," Cooper reminded him.

"As I've already pointed out—your fault to begin with, dude," Kevin replied.

"Quit fighting, you two," Gwen said. She tapped her foot impatiently. "Ben?"

"Got it!" Ben said. "Looks like you merged with a Cephalon from the planet Barlon-4."

"You mean some poor Cephalon is walking around with Cooper's arms?" Julie asked, her brown eyes wide.

Ben pressed a button, and a green light shot from the Ultrimatrix and hit Cooper. "Let's hope this works!"

Cooper's body glowed green as the Ultrimatrix repaired his DNA. By the time the light faded, he looked like his old self again.

"Whew," Cooper said. "It feels good to be back to normal again."

"If you can call that normal," Kevin said.

Gwen put her hands on her hips. "You know, Kevin, maybe you're being a little too hard on Cooper," she said. "I know this is all his fault, but he did redeem himself. It was pretty brave of him to come to your rescue."

"Yeah!" Cooper agreed.

"Maybe we could try to celebrate Cooper's birthday for real this time," Julie suggested.

Cooper looked at his watch. "It's after midnight," he said glumly. "It's not my birthday anymore."

Ben patted him on the back. "Who's counting?" he said. "Besides, Mr. Smoothie is open all night! Who's coming?"

"Me!" said Julie.

"Sure," said Gwen.

Kevin hesitated until Gwen nudged him with her elbow. "Me too," he said finally.

Grandpa Max yawned. "You kids go without me. I need my shut-eye."

They exited Plumbers HQ. As they made their way to Ben's car, he stopped and looked at the stars. Julie put an arm around him.

"What are you thinking?" she asked.

"I'm just glad Prataria and Ventulus are safe," he said. "Grandpa Max was right. The Ultrimatrix is a big responsibility. But I'm glad I have it, you know?"

Julie nodded.

Kevin stuck his head out of the car. "Hurry up, Tennyson, or I'm driving!"

Ben laughed. "No way, Kevin!"

He and Julie climbed into the car and they drove off into the night.

Somewhere in the galaxy, someone needed help.

But right now, in Bellwood, Ben Tennyson needed a smoothie.

Chapter Book #5
Chill for a Day

Turn the page for an
exclusive sneak peek at the
next Ben 10 Alien Force
chapter book!

Oh, man!" Ben Tennyson flopped forward, laying his head on his arms. "I just can't do it!"

He stayed like that for a few seconds before pushing himself upright again with a groan. Maybe if he concentrated . . .

"No way." He shook his head. "It can't be done!" He glared at the textbook on the desk in front of him. "There's just no way I can learn this chemistry in time!"

He sighed and leaned back in his chair. They had a big chemistry test in school tomorrow. And he wasn't ready. Not even close! Ben glanced at his Ultimatrix, the strange watchlike object strapped to his wrist. If only there was an alien emergency to deal with instead!

As if someone had heard him, his cell phone rang. Ben checked the number. It was his grandpa Max.

"Hey, Gramps," Ben said as he answered. "What's up?"

"Sorry to break into your study time, Ben," Max replied, "but I've picked up signs of an unannounced alien craft. It's out near the beach." Grandpa Max was one of the Plumbers, a group that monitored extraterrestrials — aliens—who came to Earth. Most of them weren't here to make new friends. But the Plumbers were mainly there to watch and negotiate. When an alien proved to be a threat, they had to turn to someone else for help. Someone like Ben.

"I'm on it!" Ben was already halfway out of his chair. "Thanks!" At last, an excuse to step away from his homework! He'd study more when he got back.

Ben considered calling his girlfriend, Julie, to see if she wanted to join him. But he knew she was studying for a biology test. Not that she'd have any trouble with it—Julie was a much better student than he was. But she probably wouldn't appreciate being disturbed. He'd fill her in tomorrow at school.

He also considered calling his cousin Gwen, and her boyfriend, Kevin. Gwen had been there with Gramps when Ben had first found the Omnitrix that let him transform into ten different alien forms. She'd developed some impressive powers of her own over the years, too, thanks to the alien blood on her grandmother's side. Kevin had once been a rival who hunted down and sold alien tech, but he'd become a good friend as well. He had his own ability—he could absorb any material just by touching it. Right now, though, Ben knew Gwen and Kevin were out on a date. Interrupting that would get him in hot water with Gwen. Ben shuddered. He didn't have an alien form tough enough to withstand his cousin's anger! Best to count them out for this one as well.

"Fine by me," Ben muttered as he headed downstairs to his sports car. "A little solo action is just what I need to wake me up." He climbed into the driver's seat, gunned the souped-up engine, and took off toward the beach.

"Okay, I'm here," Ben said softly as he pulled up by the beach and shut down the engine. "Now where are you?"

He scanned the long stretch of sand. Nothing was moving. Then a flicker of motion caught his eye. It was out over the water. Ben turned and glanced that way. There! He could just make out something—or someone—over the water a little ways out. That had to be his alien.

"So you're a flyer, are you?" Ben asked as he stepped out of the car. "No problem—I can work with that." He tapped the Ultimatrix on his wrist and the dial glowed green. As usual, the Ultimatrix read his mind and an image of the alien form he wanted appeared above it. "Let's go, Big Chill!" Ben shouted, and slammed his palm down on the figure and the Ultimatrix together.

A burst of green light washed over him and he felt the energy begin to transform him. The light faded away a second later, and Big Chill stood in Ben's place. He was tall and slender, with long, taloned hands and feet and black skin broken by bright blue patches. A pair of wide antennae rose from his squat head, above green faceted eyes and a small, almost circular mouth. Big Chill shifted his shoulders, and what had looked like a long dark cloak unfurled around him, turning into his long butterflylike wings.

"Nice night for a flight," he said in his deep, spooky voice. Then he leaped up into the air, beating his wings to gain altitude. Big Chill hovered for a second. Then he made a beeline for the unknown alien.

"Hey there!" Big Chill called out as he approached. The other alien was a race he'd never seen before, thick and heavy with short round wings in paired sets down its back and eyes mounted on long stalks. It looked like a cross between a man, a bumblebee, and a slug, especially with its mottled brown and gray coloring. But what caught Big Chill's attention was the silvery canister the alien was holding. It had the canister open and was tipping it forward. A glittering pale yellow powder was spilling out into the water!

"Okay, knock that off!" Big Chill warned, flapping up beside the stranger. The alien's eyes swiveled to stare at him, but it continued what it was doing. Unacceptable! Big Chill wasn't sure what those chemicals were, but he wasn't about to take any chances—not with the Earth's oceans!

His first thought was to use his ice-cold breath to freeze the powder. Some chemicals became dormant at lower temperatures. But it would still fall into the water, and what if it melted once it was submerged? He had to stop the powder from touching the ocean at all!

This called for something a little more than just Big Chill. This called for something—ultimate.

"Time to go ultimate," Big Chill whispered to

himself. He tapped the Omnitrix symbol on his chest, and a wave of blazing white light washed over him. He could feel himself growing larger and stronger as heat and light coursed through his body. He knew his skin was changing from blue to red as well, with fiery orange and yellow at the tips of his ears and wings. Big Chill was all about cold, but Ultimate Big Chill was fire and ice combined!

The light faded and Ultimate Big Chill dove past the stranger, shoving the canister upright. That stopped any more powder from pouring out, but what about the rest? He raced to reach the rest of the yellow powder before it could hit the water. He opened his mouth and blew hard, sending a gust of super-cold fire into the night air. The flames enveloped the glittering grains of powder and vaporized them—but Ultimate Big Chill caught a faceful of the escaping gas in the process. He gagged. Ugh, that stuff tasted terrible!

He spit out what he could and wiped at his eyes. By the time he could see clearly again, the stranger was gone!

"Oh, great," Ultimate Big Chill muttered, looking around. "Come on, where'd you go?" But he didn't see anything. The alien must have taken the opportunity to hightail it back to shore. With its brown coloring it'd be all but invisible against the sand, especially this late at night.

Ultimate Big Chill flew up and down the beach for a bit, searching, but didn't see any sign of the stranger. Well, at least he'd stopped whatever it had been planning to do to the water.

"Guess it's time to get back to studying," Ultimate Big Chill admitted as he settled back onto the ground next to his car. He willed himself back to Big Chill and then his own body—

—and nothing happened.

"What in the world?" Ultimate Big Chill tried again. He'd always been able to change back at will. A simple thought and green light would surround him again as the Ultimatrix restored him to being regular Big Chill first, followed by plain old Ben Tennyson.

But not this time.

"Oh, great." He stared at his long, clawed hands. "How am I going to explain this one?"

Gramps? You here?" Ultimate Big Chill called out as he entered the Plumbers Comm Center.

"Of course I'm here, Ben," Grandpa Max answered. He was down the hall at the computer as usual. "Why didn't you call? What happened with that alien? Holy cow!" That last was because Grandpa Max had just turned and seen Ultimate Big Chill standing there.

"Yeah," Ultimate Big Chill agreed. "'Holy cow' is right."

"What happened?" Grandpa Max asked.

"I went to check out that alien at the beach," Ultimate Big Chill explained, leaning against the desk. He had his wings folded around him like a cloak again so he wouldn't knock anything over. "It wasn't anything I've ever seen before." He described the creature.

"Hm." Grandpa Max scratched his chin. "Doesn't sound familiar, but I'll do a database search." The Plumbers kept a record of every alien species they encountered. "Did it say anything?"

"No, and I didn't give it much chance to," Ultimate Big Chill admitted. "It was dumping some kind of chemical into the water."

"That doesn't sound good."

"That's what I thought," Ultimate Big Chill agreed. "I managed to stop it, but got some of the stuff on me. It even got in my eyes. I couldn't see for a few seconds. By the time I could, the alien was gone."

"It hasn't left Earth," Grandpa Max said. "I'd have detected its ship's departure, just like I noticed its arrival. Which means it probably still has something planned. Whatever it was doing, you only stopped it for now."

"Yeah, I figured as much." Ultimate Big Chill shook his head. "Any idea what it wanted?"

"Not without knowing more about it." Grandpa Max leaned forward in his chair. "You say it got those chemicals on you?"

"Yeah." Ultimate Big Chill stood and then knelt in

front of Grandpa Max so the old man could examine him. "All over my face."

Grandpa Max studied him closely for a few minutes. "It doesn't look like there's any left," he said finally.

"No, because I washed it off as best I could," Ultimate Big Chill explained, standing up again. "I was hoping that'd help."

"Help with what?"

"With this!" Ultimate Big Chill gestured down at himself. "I can't change back, Gramps! I'm stuck this way!"

"Stuck?" Grandpa Max stared. "Did something happen to the Ultimatrix? Did it get damaged somehow?"

"No, the alien never even hit me. I shoved the canister back toward it, vaporized what had already spilled out, and got blinded. Then I was hovering over the water by myself. That was it."

Grandpa Max eyed him carefully. "Have you been messing with it again?" Ben had tried tinkering with the Omnitrix a few times over the years he had that device, in the hopes of making it more powerful. Most of those attempts had created new problems instead.

"I haven't done a thing to it!" Ultimate Big Chill insisted. And he hadn't. Ever since the Omnitrix had been upgraded to the Ultimatrix he'd been careful not to do anything but use it properly. It had been bad enough when the Omnitrix had been on the blink. It had done things like making him change forms at random. He didn't want to think about what would happen if the more powerful Ultimatrix started acting funny!

"All right, I believe you," Grandpa Max assured him. "But that means if it's not the Ultimatrix, it's Ultimate Big Chill itself." He frowned. "Something must be interfering with your body, freezing the DNA in its current shape and keeping you from changing back."

"Freezing? Do you think it's something I'm doing to myself?" Ultimate Big Chill had both fire powers and cold powers, like freezing things.

But Grandpa Max shook his head. "No, it's just an expression. I think those chemicals have locked you into this form."

"Well, that would explain this." Ultimate Big Chill stood, turned, and walked right into the desk. "Ow!"

"What was that for?" Grandpa Max asked.

"I was trying to walk through it," Ultimate Big Chill explained. Normally he could turn immaterial. But that seemed to be stuck as well.

"Hm." Grandpa Max rubbed his jaw. "Can you still turn invisible?"

"I don't know—I haven't tried." Ultimate Big Chill concentrated. After a second he felt a mild tingle and the air around him shimmered slightly. He could still see himself, but Grandpa Max started looking around. "Did it work?"

"Yep, you're invisible," Grandpa Max confirmed.

"Well, at least that's still there." Ultimate Big Chill made himself visible again. "But why invisibility and not going immaterial?"

"Maybe because turning invisible is just a trick with light waves," Grandpa Max suggested. "But going immaterial means altering your body. And right now you can't do that."

"Oh." That made sense. "Can you reverse the process?"

"Not without knowing exactly what those chemicals were and what they've done to you," Grandpa Max replied. "Otherwise I could wind up making matters worse."

"Worse?" Ultimate Big Chill stared at himself in the reflection off a computer monitor. "How could it be any worse? I look like the Moth That Ate L.A.!"

"I might get you partway back to being Ben," Grandpa Max explained. "Imagine being stuck in that body but with your own hands and feet. Or having your body but Ultimate Big Chill's head." He didn't look like he was kidding, either.

Ultimate Big Chill shivered. "No thanks! At least right now I match!" He sighed and leaned back against the desk. "Okay, now what?"

"It may just wear off on its own," Grandpa Max pointed out. "You inhaled some of the chemicals, probably, or absorbed them through your skin. Give them time to work their way out of your system."

"How long will that take?"

His grandfather shook his head. "I have no idea. I'm sorry, Ben. I'll try to think of something else, but until I know more about what did this to you there's nothing I can do."

"Great, so I'm stuck like this?" Ultimate Big Chill pulled his wings in tighter around his body, and shivered. "What do I do now?"

"Go home," Grandpa Max suggested. "You've had a rough night. Get some sleep. Study for that chemistry test. Take your mind off this. We'll find a way to fix it, I promise."

"Yeah, okay." Ultimate Big Chill pushed off of the desk. "Thanks, Gramps. Good night."

"Good night, Ben." Grandpa Max saw him out, and Ultimate Big Chill walked slowly back to his car. It took him a good five minutes to maneuver himself into the driver's seat—his wings kept snagging on the door, the steering wheel, and the dashboard. But finally he was wedged in, and he turned the key in the ignition and slowly, carefully, drove home. The last thing he needed right now was to get into an accident!

When he got home Ultimate Big Chill parked the car as best he could. Then he stumbled inside and up the stairs to his room. His chemistry textbook was still open on his desk. Ultimate Big Chill stared at it for a minute, then shook his head. He was in no mood to tackle equations and chemical formulae right now! Maybe he could cram a bit in the morning.

For now, all he wanted was to go to sleep. Hopefully he'd wake up as Ben again.

A few steps took him to his bed, and he flopped down onto it. It was late, and he was exhausted. Within seconds Ultimate Big Chill was sound asleep.